Text copyright © 2014 by Nosy Crow

Jacket art and interior illustrations copyright © 2014 by Sarah Massini

All rights reserved. Published in the United States by Random House Children's Books,

a division of Random House LLC, a Penguin Random House Company, New York.

Simultaneously published in Great Britain by Nosy Crow, Ltd., London, in 2015.

Random House and the colophon are registered trademarks of Random House LLC.

Visit us on the Web! randomhousekids.com

Educators and librarians, for a variety of teaching tools, visit us at

RHTeachersLibrarians.com

Library of Congress Cataloging-in-Publication Data

Massini, Sarah, author, illustrator.

Love always everywhere / Sarah Massini. — First edition.

   pages   cm.

Summary: "A simple look at the universality of love." —Provided by publisher.

ISBN 978-0-385-37552-8 (trade) — ISBN 978-0-375-98206-4 (ebook)

[1. Stories in rhyme. 2. Love—Fiction.] I. Title.

PZ8.3.M4212Lov 2014   [E]—dc23   2014017168

MANUFACTURED IN CHINA

10 9 8 7 6 5 4 3 2 1

First Edition

Love Always Everywhere

Sarah Massini

Random House New York

Love me

Love you

Love one

Love two

Love quiet

Love loud

Love shy

Love proud

Love lose

Love miss

Love smile

Love kiss

Love giggle

Love hug

Love tickle

Love snug

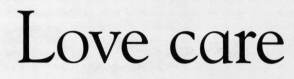

Love care

Love share

Love always . . .

. . . every

where.